NOTE TO PARENTS AND CARERS

This book is designed to put L.O.L. Surprise! fans in charge of their very own L.O.L. Surprise! adventures – and develop language and decision-making skills at the same time. Each page presents the child with different choices to make, so they can build a story, page by page. The options are endless, allowing the reader to create a new adventure each time they read the book!

When you share this book with your child, gently encourage them to take charge and make the decisions for themselves. Before they know it, they will have created their very own L.O.L. story!

HAVE FUN!

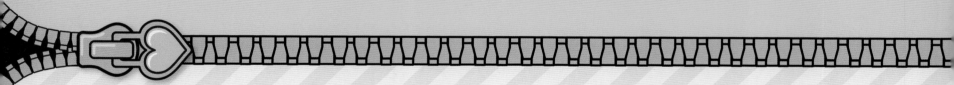

L.O.L. Surprise!: YOU DECIDE

A CENTUM BOOK 978-1-912396-59-7

Published in Great Britain by Centum Books Ltd.

This edition published 2019.

1 3 5 7 9 10 8 6 4 2

© 2019 MGA Entertainment, Inc.

L.O.L. Surprise!™ is the trademark of MGA Entertainment, Inc.

Centum Books Ltd, 20 Devon Square, Newton Abbot, Devon, TQ12 2HR, UK.

books@centumbooksltd.co.uk

CENTUM BOOKS Limited Reg. No. 07641486

A CIP catalogue record for this book is available from the British Library.

Printed in Poland.

©MGA

YOU DECIDE

centum

Have you always wanted to live a day in the life of your favourite **L.O.L. SURPRISE** doll?

SELECT A SQUAD ...

 DECIDE ON A DOLL...

CHOOSE AN ADVENTURE ...

pick **PETS, BFFs, SECRET MESSAGES**
and of course, a fabulous **DRESS CODE**
to create ...

HI BAE!

THE L.O.L SURPRISE! ADVENTURE
of your dreams!

©MGA

WELL, HERE'S YOUR **CHANCE!**

Yes, that's right - **YOU DECIDE!**

So turn the page to begin your very own **L.O.L. SURPRISE! ADVENTURE** – and the best thing is, you get to decide what happens on every page!

Even better, when you finish, you can just start all over again for more **OUTRAGEOUS FUN!**

EXCITED YET?

Every **L.O.L. SURPRISE** squad is full of amazing BFFs who can't wait to meet you!

THE GLITTERATI

ATHLETIC CLUB

GLAM CLUB

ROCK CLUB

©MGA

SLEEPOVER CLUB

S.T.E.M. CLUB

SWIM CLUB

THEATER CLUB

©MGA

Now you've selected your squad, it's time to pick your #1 BAE.

THE GLITTERATI

MADAME QUEEN, BOSS QUEEN OR INDEPENDENT QUEEN?

ATHLETIC CLUB

TOUCHDOWN, SPRINTS OR SHORT STOP?

GLAM CLUB

FLOWER CHILD, BLACK TIE OR SHOWBABY?

ROCK CLUB

PUNK BOI, GRUNGE GRRRL OR FUNKY Q.T.?

©MGA

Which L.O.L. Surprise cutie is ready for an adventure? **YOU DECIDE!**

SLEEPOVER CLUB

BABYDOLL, SLEEPING B.B. OR SLEEPY BONES?

S.T.E.M. CLUB

CAN DO BABY, VR Q.T. OR PHD B.B.?

PERFECT PICK, B.B.!

SWIM CLUB

SPF Q.T., VACAY BABAY OR RIP TIDE?

THEATER CLUB

PHARAOH BABE, ANGEL OR UNICORN?

©MGA

Every L.O.L. day is full of surprises!

Time for your beauty sleep! You're invited to a **SLEEPOVER.**

It's a vacay all day. Let's go to the **BEACH!**

It's showtime! You've got tickets to the hottest **THEATRE** show in town.

Life without ballet is pointe-less! Get yourself to **DANCE CLASS,** B.B.

What kind of outrageous adventure awaits your doll today? YOU DECIDE!

MEOW! Is your paw-fect pet best in show? Find out at the **PET SHOW.**

The Glee Club is performing the **CONCERT** of the year. Get ready to rock!

Got game? The L.O.L. Surprise basketball team needs an extra player. **JOIN THE TEAM!**

You're one smart cookie! Your super skills are needed in the L.O.L. **SCIENCE LAB.**

A perfect adventure requires the perfect outfit!

YAWN!
WHERE ARE MY PJs?

EAT, SLEEP, BEACH, REPEAT.
LET'S GET BIKINI B.B. READY.

ALL THE WORLD IS A STAGE.
BRING ME MY COSTUME!

I JUST WANT TO DANCE.
IT'S TUTU TIME!

©MGA

What's today's dress code: cool and comfy or glitter for days? YOU DECIDE!

GLAM IT UP!

THERE'S NO SUCH THING AS TOO MUCH GLITTER.

LET'S ROCK

INTO THE WEEKEND!

RIPPED JEANS ALL THE WAY.

LET'S KEEP IT SUPER CHILL.

I'VE GOTTA BE ABLE TO MOVE.

02

BEAUTY, BRAINS AND STRAIGHT As 4EVA!

SMART IS THE NEW CUTE.

It's all in the details, darling.

THE SNUGGLE IS REAL.

WAVES FOR DAYS.

DRAMA, DRAMA, DRAMA!

ALWAYS ON POINTE.

©MGA

Which accessories will make your lil' rebel's outfit POP? **YOU DECIDE!**

SPARKLE IS LIFE!

ROCK ON!

IN IT TO WIN IT.

SMARTY PANTS.

Furry friends and family make every day special!

LIL CHERRY OR CHERRY HAM?

LIL SPLASH QUEEN OR SPLASH MEOW-MAID?

LIL SUGAR OR SUGAR PUP?

LIL HONEY BUN OR BUNNY HUN?

©MGA

Can a Lil Sister tag along today or will your doll adopt a pet instead? **YOU DECIDE!**

LIL IT BABY OR IT KITTY?

LIL M.C. SWAG OR M.C. HAMMY?

LIL HOOPS M.V.P. OR HOOPS D.O.G.G.?

LIL BON BON OR HOP HOP?

No adventure is complete without a
FAB FRIEND to share it with!

PURPLE QUEEN OR STARDUST QUEEN?

HEARTBREAKER OR TROUBLEMAKER?

FOXY OR BEATNIK BABE?

FANIME OR NEON Q.T.?

©MGA

Who will be your doll's BFF 4EVA?
YOU DECIDE!

CHILLIN' WITH MY HOMIES.

SNOW ANGEL OR POSH?

TREASURE OR PRECIOUS?

D.J. OR SHORTY?

DAWN OR DUSK?

©MGA

The L.O.L. babes always have something sassy and surprising to say.

ALWAYS CLASSY AND A LITTLE SASSY!

I NEED MY BEAUTY SLEEP!

I'D RATHER BE SWIMMING.

NUTS ABOUT THE STAGE!

WHEN IN DOUBT, DANCE IT OUT.

HOW DO U LIKE MEOW?

I ROCKED B4 I COULD WALK.

I CAN CRAWL FASTER THAN YOU CAN RUN!

WHAT'S THE WIFI PASSWORD?

COUCH POTATO

BOMBSHELL

DRAMA QUEEN

DANCE LIKE NO ONE IS WATCHING

©MGA

Who is today's text message from and what does it say? **YOU DECIDE!**

LOL JK

PET LOVER

MIC CHECK

SPORTS STAR

SMART COOKIE

©MGA

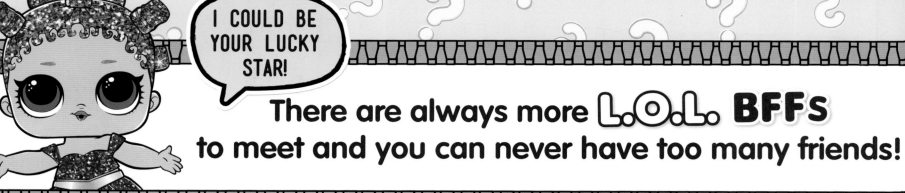

There are always more **L.O.L. BFFs** to meet and you can never have too many friends!

Which outrageous rebels will your doll bump into today? YOU DECIDE!

©MGA

The best thing about creating your own adventure is that you get to choose how it ends, too!

MAKEOVERS, MOVIES AND PLENTY OF BEAUTY SLEEP. IT WAS THE PERFECT BABES' NIGHT IN!

BATHED IN SUNSHINE AND DUSTED WITH SAND, WE SURFED UP A TOTAL STORM.

LIGHTS, CAMERA, DRAMA! TAKE A BOW, DARLING. WE WERE MADE FOR THE STAGE.

WE SHUFFLED, WE FLOSSED AND WE DANCED LIKE NO ONE WAS WATCHING!

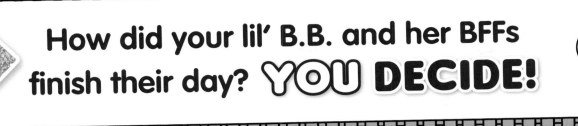

How did your lil' B.B. and her BFFs finish their day? **YOU DECIDE!**

OUR PET WAS OBVIOUSLY THE MOST ADORBS. WE WON BEST IN-SHOW, OF COURSE!

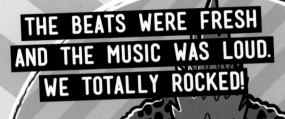

THE BEATS WERE FRESH AND THE MUSIC WAS LOUD. WE TOTALLY ROCKED!

WE DRIBBLED, DRIBBLED ... AND SCORED! SLAM DUNKS ALL THE WAY, B.B.

WE LEARNED SOMETHING NEW — LIKE WE DO EVERY DAY! THAT'S ONE GIANT LEAP FOR BABYKIND.

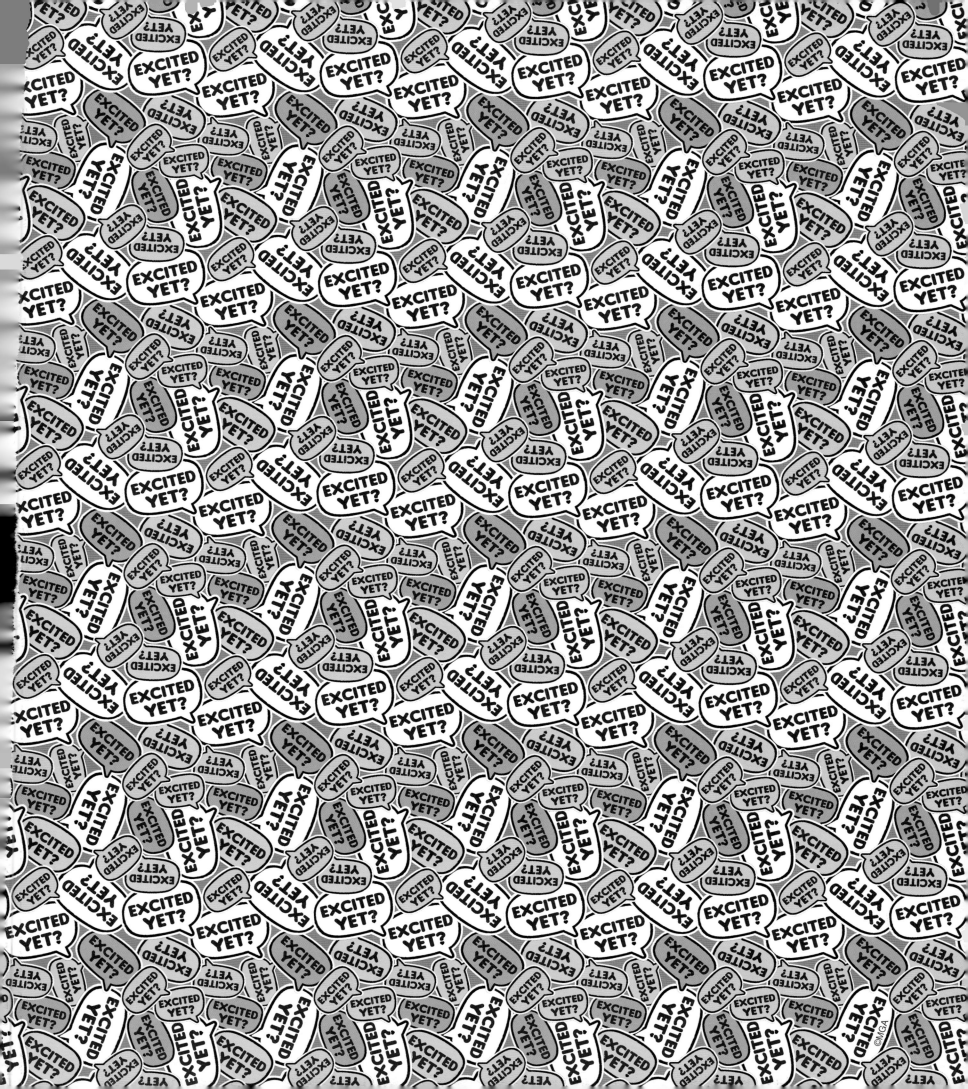

©MGA